for eating Bugs

6) Got a sweet tooth? Like candy? Waxworms are the sweetest creepy-crawly in the world.

7) Instead of an apple a day, try a stinkbug—they taste just like Granny Smiths.

8) Can't eat a mealworm? Close your eyes and pretend it's spaghetti—slurp!

9) Like PB+J? Try a PB+A for a change . . . peanut butter and ants!

10) There's a fungus among us! If you want to run faster and win a race, drink caterpillar fungus tea for a burst of energy.

Megan McDonald

Beetle McGrady Eats Bugs!

Pictures by Jane Manning

Greenwillow Books
An Imprint of HarperCollinsPublishers

Library of Congress Cataloging-in-Publication Data
McDonald, Megan.
Beetle McGrady eats bugs! / by Megan McDonald ;
pictures by Jane Manning.
p. cm.
"Greenwillow Books."
Summary: During Fun with Food Week
in her school science class,
second-grader Beetle McGrady tries to
work up the courage to eat an ant.
ISBN 0-06-001354-0 (trade).
ISBN 0-06-001355-9 (lib. bdg.)
[1. Food—Fiction. 2. Insects—Fiction. 3. Courage—Fiction.
4. Schools—Fiction.] I. Manning, Jane K., ill. II. Title.
PZ7.M478419Bd 2004 [E]—dc22 2004002107

First Edition 10 9 8 7 6 5 4 3 2

Greenwillow Books

For the McGradys—M. M.

To Mom, a brave one herself—J. M.

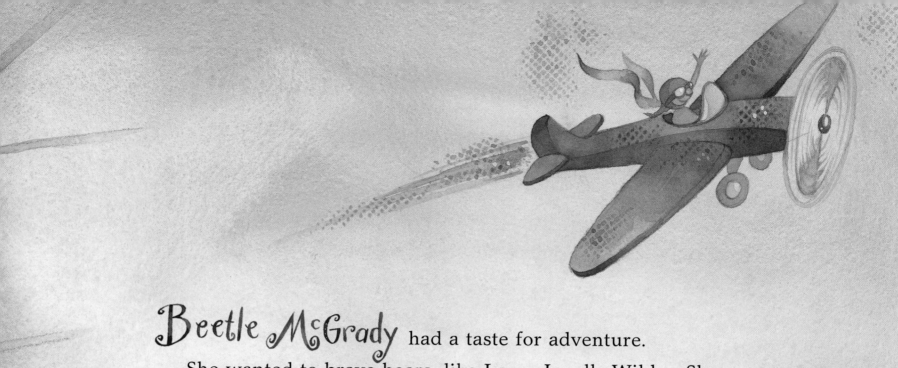

Beetle McGrady had a taste for adventure.

She wanted to brave bears, like Laura Ingalls Wilder. She wanted to sail oceans, like Marco Polo. She wanted to zoom through the skies, like Amelia Earhart. She dreamed of being a real explorer. A true pioneer.

Then came Fun with Food Week in Mr. Rigley's science class and . . . the ant.

On Monday Table Six made a food pyramid. Lacey cut out magazine pictures of artichokes. Roger drew cheese. Mona glued oatmeal cookies under "cereals" and stuck a juice box next to "fruit." Beetle found a hot dog, a hamburger, and an ant.

An ant! She could be a real explorer. A true pioneer. She, Beetle McGrady, would start her very own food group. Food group number six . . . bugs! Beetle reached to paste the ant at the top of the pyramid, but she dropped it.

"Ick! There's an ant on my artichoke!" yelled Lacey.

"EEE-yew," said Roger.

"A bug is not a food!" said Mona.

"It says here, people in Australia and Argentina eat ants for protein," Beetle said. "I bet they even eat ants as far away as ANTarctica!"

"Does it say in there to STAY AWAY from Antarctica?" asked Mona.

"I would eat an ant in a second," said Beetle.

"Prove it," said Lacey.

"Prove it," said Roger.

"Uh-oh," said Mona.

"Time to play Antarctica!" Lacey yelled on the playground.

"I'll find the ant," said Roger, crawling through the grass.

"I can't watch!" said Mona. She put on her sunglasses.

Pioneers ate boiled locusts. Explorers ate worms. Even Laura Ingalls Wilder ate cricket pie. But suddenly Beetle McGrady did not feel like a brave explorer. She did not feel like a daring pioneer. "I'm not hungry!" Beetle blurted. "I already had lunch."

"Dare double dare!" said Roger.

"Not today," Beetle told them. "Tomorrow."

At 1:07 P.M. on Tuesday, she, Beetle McGrady, would eat an ant.

Beetle practiced her ant-eating on potato chips. *Crunch.* She practiced on raisins. *Squish.* But potato chips did not crawl. And raisins did not have legs.

The next day at recess Lacey was first to catch an honest-to-goodness member of food group number six. Beetle took the ant. She closed her eyes. She, Beetle McGrady, set the itchy-twitchy, buggly-wuggly ant on the tip of her tongue.

The ant was tickly. The ant was creepy. The ant was crawly. If she ate the ant, she would be a real explorer. A true pioneer. Beetle A-for-Anteater McGrady! All she had to do was swallow. One teeny tiny gulp.

BLAHHHHH!

Beetle spit out the ant.

"Beetle can't eat an ant. Beetle can't eat an ant,"
Lacey and Roger chanted.

She, Beetle McGrady, was not an explorer.
She was not a pioneer. She was not even
Beetle A-for-Anteater McGrady.

"Don't feel bad," said Mona. "Who wants to be
best friends with an anteater?"

Fun with Food Week was not so fun anymore. On Wednesday Beetle's whole class made up a recipe for rattlesnake stew. Except Beetle. Mr. Rigley told them about a 2,000-pound popcorn ball. Beetle did not even raise an eyebrow. And when Table Six conducted an experiment on bubble gum, Beetle just chewed her pencil.

"Beetle, don't you want to chew gum in school?" asked Mona.

"*Shh!*" said Beetle. "I'm writing a poem. It's called 'The Ant Not Eaten.'"

"Oh, no. You're still thinking about that ant?"

"I want to be brave," said Beetle. "I'm about as brave as a mealworm. A mealworm is not an explorer. A mealworm is not a pioneer."

On Thursday Mr. Rigley announced, "Today we're going to explore new foods."

Beetle explored a chickpea sandwich named falafel. Roger called it awful-awful.

She ate the food of pilgrims—corn with lima beans. "Succotash gives you a rash," said Lacey.

Beetle even tasted Japanese fish eggs and Chinese bird's-nest soup. "Fish eggs smell like an art project," said Mona. "And birds' nests look like cow hair." She put on her sunglasses.

"Mr. Rigley says people risk their lives to get the nests from caves," said Beetle.

"Mr. Rigley says they're made of spit," said Mona.

It was no use. Falafel was not an ant. Succotash was not an ant. And bird's-nest soup did not make her Marco Polo. Bird's-nest soup just made her a spit eater.

inally it was Friday. A special visitor came to class.

"Second grade," said Mr. Rigley, "say hello to Chef Suzanne, from the famous restaurant Chez Chenille." Chef Suzanne unpacked dish after delicious-smelling dish.

Pork rinds? Pine nuts? "What's under those lids?" Beetle whispered.

"Ta-da!" Chef Suzanne uncovered the first plate. "All the bugs you can eat!" She picked up a toasted cricket, popped it in her mouth, *crunch*, and ate it, *glug!*

The class buzzed like bees.

"Ick!"

"Bluck!"

"Gross!"

"Yuck!"

"Sick-o!"

"Today we have Chinese chop-suey ants," said Chef Suzanne. "Mexican stinkbug salsa. Cricket pizza, from Brazil. Even super-crunch chocolate chip cookies!"

Beetle eyed the stinkbugs. The smelliest of all smellies. Tree-worm spaghetti. The squirmiest of all squirmies. Grasshopper tacos. The bugliest. But *something* smelled good. Like bacon frying. Like sweet scrambled eggs.

Beetle picked up a black witch moth caterpillar.

Beetle dangled the fried caterpillar in front of her nose.
She set the caterpillar on her tongue. She rolled it around in
her mouth. It was the awfulest of all awful-awfuls.
The cowhairiest of all cow hair. Worse than spit.

Pilots had to eat caterpillars when their planes crashed.
Beetle closed her eyes. She was Amelia Earhart on a desert
island.

Crunch, crunch, GLUG!

Beetle McGrady's
eyes rolled up.
Her tongue lolled out.
Beetle McGrady
flopped to the floor.

"Kidding!" Beetle jumped up with a smile. "Caterpillars taste like corn chips." *Munch.* "Stinkbugs taste like apples!" *Crunch!* "Crickets taste like nuts!"

"Yick! There's a cricket leg stuck in your tooth!" said Lacey.

"Gross! Bug butts and grub guts!" yelled Roger.

"Can we still have cookies if we don't eat any bugs?" asked Mona.

"Sure! Pass them around," said Chef Suzanne.

Munch! Crunch!

The cookies were extra gooey, extra crunchy.

"It's the chips," said Mona.

"It's the nuts," said Roger.

"It's the mealworms!" said Chef Suzanne.

Roger ran for the bathroom.

Lacey dashed for the trash can.

"Uh-oh," said Mona.

"Eating mealworms makes you brave," Beetle told her. She showed her friend just how to dunk a mealworm cookie into caterpillar fungus tea.

Beetle A-for-Anteater McGrady sipped and slurped her way around the world in seven bites, like an explorer, a true pioneer. And for dessert, one dozen honeypot ants.

"Today, ants. Tomorrow . . . ANTarctica!" said Beetle.

CRUNCH! CRUNCH! GLUG!

Beetle's tips

1) To help cure bad breath, bite off the rear end of a honeypot ant and chew.

2) When eating a cricket, be sure to check your smile in the mirror. "UCK! Cricket legs!"

3) ALWAYS cook tarantulas before eating. Spider fries!

4) Need a high-protein snack? Try grasshopper tacos! A serving of grasshoppers has almost as much protein as a hamburger and about half the calories. Finger-lickin' good!

5) Feeling tired? Forget to take your vitamins? Termites are full of iron.